Harvard University

# Apocrypha Concerning the Class of 1855 of Harvard College

And Their Deeds and Misdeeds during the fifteen years between July,

1865 and July, 1880

Harvard University

**Apocrypha Concerning the Class of 1855 of Harvard College**
*And Their Deeds and Misdeeds during the fifteen years between July, 1865 and July, 1880*

ISBN/EAN: 9783337178932

Printed in Europe, USA, Canada, Australia, Japan

Cover: Foto ©Andreas Hilbeck / pixelio.de

More available books at **www.hansebooks.com**

# APOCRYPHA

CONCERNING

# THE CLASS OF 1855

OF

## HARVARD COLLEGE,

AND THEIR

DEEDS AND MISDEEDS DURING THE FIFTEEN YEARS BETWEEN

JULY, 1865, AND JULY, 1880.

---

Privately Printed for the use of the Class only.

---

BY

### EDWIN H. ABBOT,

CLASS SECRETARY.

---

BOSTON:

ALFRED MUDGE & SON, PRINTERS, 34 SCHOOL STREET.

1880.

# TO THE CLASS OF 1855.

For the contents of this pamphlet the Secretary is alone responsible. If any of you think he has taken too great liberty with your story, please recollect that college life is only four years of boyhood, and that our common memories and associations are those of youth If he has erred in his effort to preserve them and their spirit, pray excuse him, for he would not willingly utter to you or of you a single unacceptable word.

According to our custom, the names of all who ever were connected with the class are embraced in this record. Among those whom circumstances early separated from us, there are some whom all would wish to claim as friends on any excuse, and there is no reason why the triennial list should circumscribe our good-fellowship.

When the Secretary sent out his first report, we were in the first flush and vigor of manhood. We have now reached the prime of life and the crown of the pathway. That out of our full number of ninety-two we have lost only fifteen during these twenty-five years is not only an illustration of the longevity of educated men, but speaks well for the temperate and manly character of our class. *Se o in cælum redeat.*

Edwin H. Abbot,
*Class Secretary.*

5 Pemberton Square, 28 June, 1880.

# MEMBERS OF THE CLASS OF 1855.

ABBOT, EDWIN HALE
AGASSIZ, ALEXANDER
ALLISON, WILLIAM
AMORY, WILLIAM
ARNOLD, LOUIS
BADGER, WILLIAM WHITTLESEY
BAILEY, JONAS MINOT
*BALCH, JOHN
BARLOW, FRANCIS CHANNING
*BARNWELL, ROBERT HAYNE
BLAKE, SAMUEL PARKMAN
BLISS, WILLARD FLAGG
BROOKS, PHILLIPS
*BROOKS, WARREN
BROWN, CHARLES LORING
BROWN, EDWARD JACKSON
BROWNE, EDWARD INGERSOLL
BUCK, CHARLES WILLIAM
BURNS, WILLIAM COLEMAN
CHACE, EDWARD HENRY
CHASE, CHARLES AUGUSTUS
CLAPP, CHANNING
CLARK, JAMES BENJAMIN
*CLARK, RANDOLPH MARSHALL
CLARKE, THOMAS WILLIAM
CROCKER, GEORGE GORDON
CUSHING, JOSEPH M.
CUTTER, CHARLES AMMI
*DALTON, EDWARD BARRY
DEXTER, GEORGE

EDGERLY, JOHN WOODS
*ELLIS, PAYSON PERRIN
EMMERTON, JAMES ARTHUR
*ERVING, LANGDON
EVANS, ALFRED DOUGLAS
EVANS, WILLIAM HENRY
EVERETT, HENRY SIDNEY
FISKE, FRANK WILLIAM
GIBBENS, EDWIN AUGUSTUS
GREEN, JOHN
GREGORY, CHARLES AUGUSTUS
GUTMAN, JOSEPH
HAMPSON, GEORGE HENRY
HAYES, JOSEPH
HEYWOOD, JOSEPH CONVERSE
HIGGINSON, HENRY LEE
HOBBS, CHARLES CUSHING
*HODGES, GEORGE FOSTER
HOSMER, JAMES KENDALL
JOHNSTON, SAMUEL
JONES, LEONARD AUGUSTUS
LAWRENCE, SAMUEL CROCKER
LONGFELLOW, WILLIAM PITT PREBLE
LYMAN, BENJAMIN SMITH
LYMAN, CHARLES FREDERIC
LYMAN, THEODORE
*MACEUEN, MALCOM
MACKAY, WILLIAM
McKENZIE, WILLIAM SLIDELL
McLELLAN, GEORGE FREDERIC

MARSH, CHRISTOPHER BRIDGE
*MERIAM, WILLIAM WARD
MITCHELL, JAMES TYNDALE
MORTON, EDWIN
PAINE, ROBERT TREAT
*PERKINS, STEPHEN GEORGE
PHILBRICK, WILLIAM DEAN
PHILLIPS, WILLARD QUINCY
RAND, EDWARD SPRAGUE
REED, JAMES
RICHARDS, WILLIAM WHITING
RIDDLE, WILLIAM QUINCY
ROPES, NATHANIEL
RUPPANNER, ANTOINE
*RUSSELL, EDWARD GRENVILLE
RUSSELL, GEORGE PEABODY

SANBORN, FRANKLIN BENJAMIN
*SANGER, CHARLES FREDERIC
SAWYER, GEORGE CARLETON
*SCHLEY, SAMUEL RINGGOLD
SEAWELL, JAMES MANY
STONE, CHARLES FRANCIS
THWING, EDWARD PAYSON
TILESTON, JOHN BOIES
VENTRES, WILLIAM HOSMER SHAILER
*WAINWRIGHT, ISAAC PARKER
WALKER, HENRY
WATERS, HENRY FITZ GILBERT
WILD, WALTER HENRY
WILLARD, JOSEPH
WRIGHT, SMITH
YONGUE, ANDREW LAMMEY

# HARVARD COLLEGE

## CLASS OF 1855.

EDWIN H. ABBOT was married Sept. 19, 1866, to Martha T., the youngest daughter of the late Eben Steele, Esq , of Portland, Me. His only son. Philip Stanley Abbot, was born in Brookline. Mass , on Sept. 1, 1867. He spent three months in the Azores in 1869, but, with that exception, was constantly engaged in the practice of law in Boston, at No. 4 Court Street and No. 13 Pemberton Square, from 1867 to July, 1875. in partnership with Leonard A. Jones. Since July, 1875, he has had no partner. Since 1873, he has been employed in railroad and corporate litigation and affairs ; and, since 1875, has maintained an office in Milwaukee, Wis., at No. 110 Wisconsin Street, as well as in Boston. His present Boston office is at No. 5 Pemberton Square. He has practised, chiefly in the Federal courts, in many States as well as in the United States Supreme Court in Washington. In 1878, he was appointed to succeed the late Chief Justice George T. Bigelow, as Trustee under the first mortgage of the Wisconsin Central Railroad Company. As the active Trustee in possession of that railroad during the past eighteen months, he has been reorganizing it upon a novel plan, which is truly styled a new departure in corporate reorganization. It avoids the losses incident to ordinary foreclosures, and has, therefore, attracted considerable attention from many persons who have been so unfortunate as to be interested in such property during the recent hard times. He may be addressed, indifferently, either at Milwaukee, or Post-office Box No. 1,151,

Boston. He still maintains his citizenship in Cambridge, Mass., where he built a house on the site of the "Charles C. Little" observatory, but gave it up to become commorant in Wisconsin, and live in Pullman cars. He is the General Solicitor and Vice-President of the reorganized Wisconsin Central Railroad Company. So far as official duties permit, he accepts retainers in corporate and chancery causes. This class of litigation in the West is chiefly confined to the Federal courts; and he consequently wanders over the West and the Northwest generally. Indeed, the only limit to his travels is set by the amount of the retainer. His latest and toughest case has been the preparation of these APOCRYPHA concerning his classmates.

ALEXANDER AGASSIZ started on a deep-sea dredging trip early in the present month of June. He wrote the Secretary that he was very sorry to miss our dinner, and greatly feared that, while we were eating ours, he would be getting rid of his. This ante-peristaltic action seemed as unpleasing in prospect to our great *savant* as we unscientific "*ignorami*" find it actually to be. Not even his perfect comprehension of the process reconciles him to its use. Nevertheless, to the thoughtful mind, here is beautifully exhibited the exquisite economy of nature. As thus: he whose genius dissects the minute natives of the ocean, is compelled to nourish the wondrous, little beasts on which that genius feeds. While by his mental processes he illustrates the structure of his specimens, he, at the same time, in accordance with the law of evolution, by a simple natural function, helps to keep up the supply. Thus the man supports the Curator, and we behold the survival of the fittest, and the powers of destruction and construction working together.

Agassiz's children since 1865 are Maximilian Agassiz, born May 21, 1866, and Rudolphe Louis Agassiz, born Sept. 3, 1871. In 1874, he suffered the double loss of both father and wife; and much as he doubtless knew of friendly sympathy then, he could not know, though he might feel, the influence of the general sorrow of friends and neighbors, who did not think it kind to press it upon his notice.

To Agassiz belongs the honor of having the first boy of "1855" in Harvard College. His oldest son is at this moment a member of the class of 1884, having in 1879 passed his examination.

In 1865, Agassiz became engaged in coal mining in Pennsylvania, in addition to his occupation at the Zoölogical Museum. This led to his going to Lake Superior in 1866, and being connected with the Calumet Mine, first, as its treasurer, and, afterwards, in 1867, as the superintendent of that and the adjoining mine, the "Hecla." He lived with his family two years and a half on Lake Superior; and then returned to Boston to become the president of the company, which office he has retained to the present day.

In the fall of 1869, he visited Europe and examined the museums and collections of England, France, Germany, Italy, and Northern Europe. He returned in the fall of 1870, and resumed his duties as Assistant Curator of the museum. Upon the death of Professor Louis Agassiz in 1874, he was appointed Curator, which office he still holds; and he assures the Secretary that he regularly draws the large salary connected with that office. During the summer of 1874, he acted as Director of the Anderson School of Natural History at Penikese. Differences between Mr. Anderson and the Director led to the closing of this school at the end of its second session.

In 1875, he made an expedition to the west coast of South America, to examine the copper mines of Peru and Chili. During that time he made an extended survey of Lake Titicaca, and with the aid of his assistant, Mr. Sarman, gathered an immense collection of Peruvian antiquities, which is now in the Peabody Museum at Cambridge. These collections represent the antiquities of the Lake of old Trahuanaco, and of the shore Indians at Ancon.

In 1875, he was invited by Sir Wyville Thomson to assist him in arranging and making up the collections of the great, English exploring expedition of the "Challenger," and a part of these collections he brought back with him from Scotland to this country. He has just finished his final report on the sea-urchins of this famous expedition.

Since 1876, he has himself spent every winter in similar deep-sea dredging expeditions, the superintendent of the Coast Survey having each year placed at his disposal the steamer "Blake." These

2

expeditions have enabled him to explore the deep water of the Gulf of Mexico and of the Caribbean Sea. The success which has attended these expeditions has been very considerable, mainly, as *he* says, from the interest shown in the work by the commanders of the " Blake"; but very much, as I am assured by others, through his own great ingenuity and special familiarity with hoisting and mining machinery, which has enabled him to introduce new methods in place of the old ways of deep-sea dredging.

" I have less hair," he writes, " than I had twenty years ago, but have lost no teeth, and am neither blind nor gouty."

Agassiz's remarkable skill and success in Lake Superior copper-mining is absolutely unique. It is fair to tell his classmates, what is the simple truth, that the development of the Calumet and Hecla mines, which supply annually one tenth of all the copper used in the civilized world, and control the American market, is more the result of his scientific and executive ability than of any other one thing. Its plant of machinery alone has cost over $3,000,000. It has been devised and created under his direct supervision, and has rendered these mines, *par excellence*, second to none in the world. For most men this mining achievement would alone be a life-work, and glory enough to make its author famous. To Agassiz, however, it is merely an incident in a scientific life, which already has placed him in the front rank of natural scientists.

As a single illustration of the noble way in which he uses his great wealth in public enterprises, a quotation from the history of Alma Mater will please you. What generous acts in the by-ways of private life such a man performs, may be conjectured from this story; but silence is here the most genuine tribute of respect.

President Eliot, in his speech at the annual dinner of the Harvard Club in New York, Feb. 20, 1880, made the following remarks: —

" I said that I hardly knew myself how much money the University has received. Let me give you an illustration of the difficulties which I encounter in trying to add up the gifts to the University. One of our most liberal benefactors has given since 1871 *no less than* $230,000 *to a single department of the University,* besides numerous subscriptions and gifts to other departments. The public knows of this gentleman's beneficence to the College only to the amount of $65,000. He has a peculiar way of giving. He sees a need in one of the departments of the University, and he goes and supplies it, pays the bill, and says nothing about the transaction. He thinks this department needs more room. He contracts for a building and erects it on the land of the President and Fellows, without even communicating the fact that he proposes to erect such a building. In this way he has given the University $230,000. These facts have been heretofore unknown except to two or three persons; but it seemed to me they were very instructive, and that you would like to hear them.

"As this gentleman is sitting at your table, I will not wound his modesty by mentioning his name: but I will take the liberty of mentioning that he is a distinguished scientific student and author, the best authority in the world on certain forms of marine life, and an indefatigable explorer of the depths of the sea; that he was formerly an Overseer, and is now a Fellow, of the corporation; and that he is, incidentally, the manager of the most successful copper mine in the world."

Your Secretary procured, with extreme difficulty, from the learned author, a list of Agassiz's publications. But this eminent *savant* indulges in a chirography which is simply vile. The Secretary's science is now so slight that, as soon as the MSS. arrived, he promptly sent them, upon mere inspection of the record, travelling two thousand miles after the Fish Commissioner for translation into that cursive character which printers love. If the learned author finds his little beasts nicknamed, the Secretary avers that all errors in their titles are due to the crass ignorance of the fishy translation, and the probable use of a lame pony by some piscatorial hireling. The Secretary solemnly affirms that *he* did not venture to tamper with a single letter even in the name of that single familiar creature, of which, in his boyhood, he made the acquaintance off the wharves of Beverly. The department of Fish must bear the responsibility.

PUBLICATIONS OF AGASSIZ.

*In the Proceedings of the Boston Society of Natural History,*
*1866–1869.*

On Salpa Cabotti. Vol. XI. 1866.

Notes on Beaver Dams. 1869.

Habits of Echinoderms. 1869.

On Sandstones of Lake Superior.

*In the Annals of the Lyceum of Natural History, 1866-1869.*

Arachnactis brachiolata.

Embryology of Starfishes (Tornaria).

Young stages of a few Annelids (reprinted from Ann. Mag. Nat. Hist.).

Notes on the genus Leskia of Lovén.

*In the Proceedings of the American Academy of Arts and Sciences,*
*1874–1878.*

Notice of Dr. J. E. Holbrook.

Hydrographic sketch of Lake Titicaca. Echini from Kerguelen Island.

Sketch of Von Baer.

On the young of Osseous Fishes. I.

On the young of Osseous Fishes. II. Development of the Flounders.

Embryology of Lepidosteus.

*In the Memoirs of the American Academy, 1872.*

Embryology of Balanoglossus and Tornaria.

Embryology of Ctenophoræ.

*In the American Naturalist, 1872–1876.*

Reviews of " Huxley and Martin's Biology."

Lankester on Limulus.

Note on Tornaria.

Note on Arachnactis.

Note on Flounders.

On Zoölogical Stations.

On Delesse Lithology of deep sea.

On Pedicellariæ.

On Zoölogical Nomenclature.

In *Nation* and in *Nature*, a number of reviews on Haeckel, deep-sea dredging expeditions, and other zoölogical subjects; a review of the " Life of J. D. Forbes."

### In the American Journal of Science.

A number of reviews and minor papers.

On Haeckel's " Allacogenesis."

Milne Edwards's " Oiseaux Fossils."

Thomson's " Depths of the Sea."

Progress in the Natural History of Annelids.

Claparède's " Bryozoa."

Notice of Claparède.

Metschinkoff on Comatula.

Allman's " Tubularia."

Reviews of papers by Kewalewky, Metschinkoff, and Leuckart.

Notice of the Habits of young Limulus.

The Gastræa Theory of Haeckel.

Haeckel's " System der Medusen."

Instinct in Hermit Crabs.

### In the Archives de Zoölogie, 1875–1879.

Development des Pleuronectes.

Hybridité des Étoiles de Mer.

Sur les Edwardsies.

Les Théories Embryogéniques de Haeckel.

Report of the Anderson School of Penikese, 1873.

Reports of the Museum of Comparative Zoölogy for 1873, 1874, 1875, 1876, 1877, 1878, 1879.

14

*In the Bulletins of the Museum of Comparative Zoölogy.*
1869–1879.

Echini collected by Mr. Pourtalés in the Gulf Stream, and Addenda to the same, with List of Starfishes.
New species of Echini.
Preliminary Notice of the "Hassler" Echini.
The Carboniferous Belt of Lake Titicaca.
Corals from Tilibiche, Peru, by A. Agassiz and L. F. Pourtalés.
Application of Photography to Natural History.
Letters 1 to 3 on the Dredging Expeditions of the U. S. Coast Survey Steamer "Blake," to Superintendent of U. S. Coast Survey.

*In the Memoirs of the Museum of Comparative Zoölogy,*
1872–1877.

Revision of the Echini.
Echini of the "Hassler" Expedition.
North American Starfishes.

PRIZES.

*From the Boston Society of Natural History.*

Walker Prize of Natural History.
The Grand Honorary Prize, given once in five years, was in 1873 given to A. Agassiz, first time it had been given.

*From the Academie des Sciences of Paris.*

The Prix Serres, given once in ten years, was in 1878 for the first time assigned to a foreigner, — to A. Agassiz.

He was appointed Curator of the Museum of Comparative Zoology in 1874, and Director of the Anderson School of Natural History in 1874. He was elected by the Alumni one of the Overseers of Harvard College in 1874, and was chosen by the corporation to be one of the Fellows of Harvard College in 1878.

He is also a member of the following societies: The Academy of Natural Sciences, Philadelphia, and the American Philosophical

Society of the same place ; the Essex Institute, Salem, Mass. ; the National Academy of Science of the United States ; the Société Philomatique, Paris ; the American Association for the Advancement of Science ; the Société Helvétique des Sciences Naturelles ; Senckenbergische Gesellschaft, Frankfort ; Société des Sciences Naturelles, Chérbourg ; the Society of Natural History of Montreal ; the Geological Society of Manchester ; the Zoölogical Society of London ; the Linnean Society, London ; the Literary and Philosophical Society, Liverpool ; Société Impériale des Naturalistes de Moscow ; Physik Med. Gesellschaft, Würzburg ; the Society of Mining and Mechanical Engineers ; " Isis," of Dresden ; Academia Panormitana ; Naturforschende Gesellschaft of Emden ; Verein für Vaterländische Cultur, Würtemberg ; Royal Microscopical Society of London ; Société de Physique et d'Histoire Naturelle de Genève.

**WILLIAM ALLISON.** Nothing has been heard about Allison by the Secretary since the last report in 1865.

**WILLIAM AMORY, Jr.** Amory has continued in business in Boston since the last report. He is a member of the firm of J. L. Bremer & Co., and resides at No. 29 Chestnut Street, Boston.

**LOUIS ARNOLD.** He has lived a very quiet and monotonous life, he says, since 1865. In January, 1865, he entered the office of Campbell, Whittier & Co., makers of steam engines, boilers, general machinery, and elevators, which were then just coming into demand for buildings. He intended to remain for three months only to adjust their accounts, which were then somewhat demoralized. He has continued, however, in that business ever since, and is now a part owner in the Whittier Machinery Company, the successor of Campbell, Whittier & Co., and a corporation organized under the laws of Massachusetts. He finds the business pleasant in its nature. The enormous demand for elevators in public buildings and private residences has made the manufacture of elevators a very important item in his business. He has made two for Agassiz, and seven for E. I. Browne, and is making boilers for the class generally. He frequently sends boilers to the West. His concern makes more varieties of elevators than any other factory. They had one in the late Sydney exhibition in Australia. It was the object of special mention, and received a special award. Arnold's duties embrace accounts and the keeping the time of one hundred and thirty employés, and tabulating material used in the construction of various machines, and in estimating the cost of each. This work is the more important and difficult because no two elevators are alike; and he consequently finds his mathematical training at Harvard of the greatest value.

On May 8, 1866, he was married in Providence to Helen Adelia Nichols. History records that his marriage presented such peculiar difficulties that it took two clergymen to surmount them, — one an Episcopalian and the other a Baptist. The actual performance resulted in a quarrel between these two representatives of Christianity, which added a peculiar spiciness to the occasion. He has had three children : the eldest, Ethel Hastings, born April 27, 1868 ; Chester, born May 1, 1870; and Evelyn Howard, born Oct. 27, 1875. His youngest little girl died suddenly during Arnold's absence at the Exposition at Philadelphia. Arnold means that his boy shall go to Harvard.

WILLIAM WHITTLESEY BADGER is still practising law in New York City, having his office at No. 178 Broadway, and waiting impatiently for the publication of the College "Roll of Honor."

JONAS MINOT BAILEY. Nothing has been heard from Bailey since our graduation.

* JOHN BALCH. Died in Somerville many years ago.

FRANCIS CHANNING BARLOW resumed the practice of law in New York City at the close of the war. He was appointed United States Marshal by President Grant; and his independent conduct of that office, and refusal to pay political assessments based upon a valuation of its assumed corrupt use, led to a spicy correspondence in the *Nation*, which honest men greatly enjoyed, and which reflected honor on Barlow's old instructors in rhetoric. At the last moment before going to press, the Secretary has received from Boston the following model letter in reply to his circular. It speaks for itself; and no apology is necessary for printing it at length. His firm is Barlow & Olney, having its office at No. 206 Broadway.

" NEW YORK, 206 BROADWAY, June 20, 1880.

EDWIN H. ABBOT, Esq., *Class Secretary*.

" *My Dear Abbot*, — At your request I write an account of the principal events of my life since our decennial class meeting in 1865.

" It is not agreeable to speak of one's self, and I therefore make my story as brief as possible.

" In the fall of 1865 I returned to Massachusetts from the army, somewhat uncertain whether I should resume the practice of the law in the city of New York, or go South in some commercial or industrial pursuit, or perhaps even remain in the army, where Mr. Stanton had personally offered me a good rank.

" In September, 1865, I was unexpectedly nominated (while I was still in Massachusetts) for the office of Secretary of State by the New York Convention. A military candidate was desired, and I happened to be the most available candidate of high rank.

" The Democrats nominated Gen. Slocum, a distinguished officer, but our ticket was elected.

" On the day after election, — that is, on Nov. 7, 1865, — I resigned my commission as Attorney-General.

" This nomination and election determined me to return to New York, and to my profession, the law.

" My term of office began on Jan. 1, 1866, and lasted two years, my office and official residence being at Albany.

" The office, though next to that of Lieutenant-Governor (and consequently the third office in the State) in nominal rank, is in its own proper duties an insignificant one. But as a member of the Canal Board, and one of the Commissioners of the Canal Fund (which has a supervision of canal affairs), and a Commissioner of the Land Office, which has charge of the public lands, the Secretary has important duties and responsibilities.

3

" The recollection of this office gives me little satisfaction.

" Some of my colleagues and myself opposed, as well as we could, the corrupt canal schemes which have disgraced the State, but we were not sufficiently acquainted with the subject to be of much public service, and altogether I did but little good.

" Finding that I was not required to be at Albany the entire time, I resumed the practice of the law in New York, opening an office there on May 15, 1866.

" By a piece of great good luck, I obtained the position of counsel of the National Park Bank, one of the two largest banks in the country, in the size of its deposits and the volume of its business.

" This client I have always retained ; and, as it has an immense foreign (out-of-town) correspondence, it has been of great value professionally.

" During 1866 and 1867, I spent about half of the time at Albany, and half in my office in New York.

" I was not renominated for Secretary, although I was a candidate.

" The convention was in the hands of the faction of the party, the Fenton wing, to which all the outgoing State officers were opposed, and none of us were renominated.

" The Democrats were, however, successful at the election.

" I continued the practice of my profession, without holding any political office, until May, 1869, when I was appointed by General Grant to be United States Marshal for the Southern District of New York.

" I held this office until October of that year (1869), when I resigned, because the duties of the office broke up my professional practice, which was worth far more than $6,000, the pay of the Marshal, or rather the *honest* salary.

" I feel great satisfaction in my discharge of the duties of this office.

" It had become a nest of corruption, plundering the litigants in the Federal courts (whose sheriff or executive officer the Marshal is), and being mixed up with the great frauds then perpetrated on the United States revenue, in connection with the whiskey and tobacco excise.

" In less than a week I removed every person whom I found in
the office, and supplied their places by honest and faithful officers,
and introduced a high degree of discipline and efficiency.

" In the summer of 1869, strenuous attempts were made by sym-
pathizers with the Cuban insurgents to send men, arms, and supplies to that island, which expeditions the government sought to
suppress, as being violations of the neutrality laws.

" The duty of breaking up these expeditions fell upon me, and, in
connection with the United States Attorney, I was invested by the
President (by an especial commission under the Act of 1818) with
extraordinary powers over the United States forces — military,
naval, and revenue — in New England, New York, and New Jersey. For several months our operations were very like those of
a military and naval campaign, and we captured large numbers
and amounts of men and materials of war, and completely broke
up these expeditions.

" When these operations were over I resigned, as above stated,
procuring from the President the appointment of my chief deputy
as my successor.

" Early in 1871 I had an experience of a *quasi* public character,
which I mention because it probably had some influence in procuring my nomination as Attorney-General.

" In that spring I was one of the founders of the ' Bar Association,' the first institution of the kind in the country, and for the
first two years I was one of its Executive Committee.

" In February of that year (1871) I had a public controversy
(through a series of letters to the *Tribune*) with Mr. David Dudley
Field, as to his connection with Fisk and Gould and the Erie Railway, which I vehemently attacked. This involved criticisms of
Judges Barnard and Cardozo, then on the bench, and in the height
of their power ; and the controversy was of public service as showing
that a member of the Bar, practising before them, might publicly
attack them and their acts without incurring any serious risks.

" At the conclusion of this controversy I preferred charges in
the Bar Association against Mr. Field, which went off on the tech-
nical ground that the acts complained of were done before he
became a member of the Association.

"On the 4th of July, 1871, the so-called 'Tweed,' or 'Ring' disclosures were made, and I was appointed one of the 'Committee of Seventy,' which was appointed by the citizens of all parties to further the cause of reform.

"I was made Chairman of its Law Committee, and afterwards one of its four paid counsel.

"In September, 1871, I was nominated by the Republicans for the office of Attorney-General. This was no doubt owing to my connection with the Committee of Seventy, and also to my controversy with Mr. Field, and the attention which had been attracted to it.

"I was elected, and held the office through 1872 and 1873.

"As Attorney-General, I had the superintendence of all the suits and prosecutions against Tweed and the other ring peculators, the active management of which was conducted by Mr. O'Conor and Mr. Tilden, and other counsel retained and paid by me (except Mr. O'Conor and Mr. Tilden, who would receive no compensation).

"I also brought the suit in the name of The People, and conducted the proceedings, against Fisk and Gould, which resulted in their being ousted from control of the Erie Railway.

"But my chief personal exertions in this office were in connection with canal matters.

"I made myself thoroughly familiar with the laws on this subject, and with canal matters generally.

"I opposed every corrupt scheme in the Canal Board, not only by my vote and influence, but also by bringing suits in the name of The People, and procuring injunctions against my colleagues and others.

"I also brought a large number of suits to recover money corruptly obtained from the State, besides checking many payments by injunction and otherwise.

"Some forms of corruption were entirely checked during my term of office.

"I feel that I thoroughly and efficiently discharged my duty as Attorney-General.

"My suits and proceedings were generally successful in the Supreme Court, but ultimately failed by decisions of the Court of Appeals. Most of the suits tried in the time of Mr. Tilden's governorship, and since, after his ' canal reform policy ' had attracted attention, were originally brought by me. Of a list of fourteen, lately reported to the Legislature as constituting the ' Canal Reform ' litigations, all but three — that is, eleven — were brought by me.

" Although these suits have generally failed in the Court of Appeals, as above stated, they were of service as attracting attention to canal peculations, and as exposing these frauds in the courts. Although little, if anything, has been recovered from the peculators, yet the agitation has resulted in stopping these peculations, and in constitutional amendments which have rendered them far more difficult.

" I have the satisfaction of knowing that, of the jobs and schemes which Mr. Tilden's Canal Investigating Committee brought to public attention and condemnation, every one which came before the Canal Board appears by its records to have met my vigorous opposition and condemnation. I was not renominated for this office. I early refused to be a candidate ; but about two weeks before the convention I consented, at the request of Governor Dix, Mr. O'Conor, Mr. Evarts, and others, that my name might be used. But it was too late to accomplish anything in the convention, even if an earlier movement on my part would have been effectual against the hostility of the canal and ring peculators.

" Since Jan. 1, 1874, I have held no public office, but have practised my profession, which I had continued, as best I could, through the periods of public office above mentioned.

" While I was Attorney-General, however, I was able to do but little in my private office, being kept at Albany most of the time.

" I have always practised in the city of New York ; and since 1870 I have been in partnership with Mr. Peter B. Olney, a graduate of Harvard in the Class of 1864, my firm being Barlow & Olney.

" My practice, though not brilliant or as lucrative as I might wish, has been respectable and comfortable.

" My clients have been largely banks, bankers, and corporations, many of them coming to me through the Park Bank.

" Of late years I have been largely occupied as counsel of the receivers of insolvent savings banks and insurance companies, and in that capacity I have had large experience in suits of rather a novel character, — that is, suits against trustees and officers of these institutions, to recover money lost by their illegal and improper acts; and we have succeeded in establishing principles which hold such persons to a strict performance of their duties.

"I have also been retained somewhat by the city and State authorities in suits against public officers, or relating to public affairs.

" This latter business, as well as the savings-bank and insurance business, grew out of my having held the office of Attorney-General, which has thus resulted in an incidental advantage to me.

" Since I was Attorney-General I have been engaged in one matter of a quasi-public nature.

" After the Presidential election of 1876, I was asked by General Grant, then President, to go to Florida to ' witness the count.'

" I had the misfortune to differ from most of my party as to the result in Florida, and I frankly expressed my opinion. I supposed that we were asked to visit the disputed States, not as ' counsel ' for the Republican party, but as impartial and disinterested observers whose honest opinion was desired. I acted strictly in that capacity, and labored faithfully, not only to urge the case of the Republicans where I believed they were right, but to equally protect the rights of the other side, and to have the result declared in accordance with law and justice, as I understood them.

" For this I have been accused of treachery to the Republican party, but no question was ever made to me as to the propriety of my position and conduct (even by those who now bitterly attack them) while we were in Florida or on our way home, or afterwards (I having received friendly communications from some of the chief of my critics after our return home), until three years had elapsed. I have at least the satisfaction of being satisfied with the integrity of my own conduct; for I believe that no evils which can possibly result from the ascendency of the Democratic party (and as a strong and unfaltering Republican I believe that those evils would be very great) would be so ruinous as the adoption by the Republican party of the practice of cheating at Presidential elections.

"In October, 1866, I was married to Miss Ellen Shaw, of Staten Island, the youngest daughter of Francis George Shaw, Esq., and the sister of Col. Robert G. Shaw, whom I fitted to enter the Sophomore Class, at Harvard, in the summer of 1856. My wife's next eldest sister is the widow of Col. Charles Russell Lowell, of the Class of 1854. Her two other sisters married respectively Mr. George William Curtis and Mr. Robert B. Minturn. I have three children, — two sons and one daughter. The oldest, Robert Shaw Barlow, was born July 4, 1869, at Staten Island ; the second son, Charles Lowell Barlow, was born in the city of New York, on Oct. 10, 1871 ; and the girl at Lenox, Mass., on July 27, 1873, her name being Louisa Shaw Barlow.

"Since 1865 I have lived in the city of New York, except that I pass my summers (or rather my family do) at Lenox, Mass.

"This letter is not as brief as I expected when I began, and I fear it is much longer and fuller than most of those which you have received. However, as I write at the last moment of the time which you have given us, I have no time to rewrite or condense it. I have necessarily spoken without reserve of myself, because if these autobiographies are to be of any value at all as giving an insight into the lives of the class, it is necessary that we should speak frankly and without hesitation.

"Ever sincerely your classmate,

"FRANCIS C. BARLOW."

* ROBERT HAYNE BARNWELL, probably, died in South Carolina some years ago. The Secretary is unable to obtain authentic information with regard to him.

SAMUEL PARKMAN BLAKE, JR., married Oct. 14, 1868, Miss Mary Lee Higginson, sister of our classmate, and removed from Philadelphia to Boston with his family in 1872, and entered into the real-estate business. His present office is No. 19 Exchange Place. He resides at No. 32 Chestnut Street, Boston, and has four children : Marion Lee, born July 11, 1869 ; Robert Parkman, born Oct. 26, 1870 ; Theresa Huntington, born Jan. 12, 1874 ; George Higginson, born April 23, 1876.

WILLARD FLAGG BLISS. Nothing has been heard from Bliss for many years, but he is supposed to be married and farming in Illinois.

PHILLIPS BROOKS. In the autumn of 1869 he left Philadelphia, where he had been living for ten years, and came to Boston to be the rector of Trinity Church. He spends this summer in England, and regrets that he is compelled to leave before the date of our dinner. He lives at 175 Marlboro Street. Brooks soon found the old edifice on Summer Street too small for his congregation; and when the great fire destroyed it in 1872, the parish built on the Back Bay the largest and finest church in Boston. It is crowded at every service; and several of his classmates are among those who throng it to listen to his words about the only life worth living, and to get help from him to live it. It is not easy to express what should be said about him here, because to say the whole truth would seem extravagant. His power in the pulpit is, actually, one of the great forces which exist and act to-day in shaping human life in our city; and in more than our city. No one can sit under his preaching and help feeling that its soul lies in the preacher's own efforts to be himself what he urges and helps others to become. Never was a prophet more honored and revered by those who knew him, though he dwells in his own country; and none more freely and heartily recognize and accept him in his function than his own classmates and old schoolmates.

He generally spends the summer in Europe to rest and prepare for the next season's work. He has preached often in England, where he is followed almost as he is here. He holds a special service, and preaches on July Fourth of this year in Westminster, by Dean Stanley's invitation, as he has already done in former years. As we grow older and learn to seek more for the substance and care less for the shadows of human existence, Brooks becomes to those who were boys with him more and more a friend. The ties which drew them to him in youth are twisted into the fibre of their best aspirations in maturer years, and reach down into the secret chambers of their lives.

\* WARREN BROOKS died at Townsend, Mass., on Feb. 4, 1857.

CHARLES LORING BROWN. Nothing has been heard of Brown since he left us in the Freshman year.

EDWARD JACKSON BROWN was, at the time of the last report, a prosperous merchant in the firm of Bemis & Brown, manufacturers and jobbers of cotton goods in St. Louis, Mo., and dealers in cotton in Boston. About 1873, he withdrew from this firm, after it had lasted for about sixteen years. Rumor says the reason of its dissolution was that both partners had grown so rich that they were too lazy to make any more money. Since that time, Brown has courted fortune in a desultory way, keeping up his shingle, he says, as a dealer in cotton, in association with his brother, under the firm name of E. J. Brown & Co. But he hardly commends his example to any aspiring young merchant who wishes to do business. He denies the existence of any literary bantlings, and has always avoided foreign travel. He has had six children : Charles Farwell, who was born Jan. 20, 1865, and died Nov. 16, 1877 ; Edward Lyman, born March 25, 1867 ; Walter Jackson, born Oct. 5, 1870 ; Frederick Hamilton, born March 15, 1873 ; Mary Louise, born Oct. 12, 1875 ; Winthrop Holman, who was born Nov. 12, 1878, and died in infancy.

EDWARD I. BROWNE thinks he has no history to relate. This is partly explained by the fact that he is still unmarried. But all of us in Boston are familiar with his reputation as a trustee and custodian of property. He has been associated for several years in his business with Charles Thorndike. The office of Browne & Thorndike is No. 47 State Street. Browne is now one of the trustees of the Francis estate ; and those of us who have families hope, for the sake of those we love best, that Browne will long survive us. His house is No. 52 Commonwealth Avenue.

CHARLES WILLIAM BUCK resided for some years in Portland, Me., as pastor of the Unitarian Church in that city. His present abode is unknown to the Secretary.

4

WILLIAM COLEMAN BURNS is said to be in Europe, and his probable address is, care of Messrs. J. S. Morgan & Co., Paris.

EDWARD HENRY CHACE. Nothing has been heard from Chace since our graduation.

CHARLES A. CHASE succeeded his father as Treasurer of Worcester County in 1865. He held that office until January, 1876, when he was elected Register of Deeds, which office he held until 1877. For the next three years he served as the Secretary of the Board of Trade, and in 1879 superintended the establishment of a successful telephone exchange. In the summer of 1879, he wrote "The History of Worcester" (120 pages royal octavo) for "The History of Worcester County," published by C. J. Jewett & Co., of Boston. In November last he was elected Treasurer of the Worcester Institution for Savings, with which he had been connected for several years as trustee, Auditor, and member of the Board of Investment. He has two children: Mary Alice, born Oct. 10, 1865, and Maud Eliza, born Sept. 2, 1867.

CHANNING CLAPP, at the close of the war in 1865, went on a plantation in Georgia, near Savannah. In 1867 he engaged in business in New Orleans, where he remained during the winters of ten years, spending the summer at the North. He was married in 1869, and returned to Boston in 1877, where he has since resided. He has dealt in cotton.

JAMES BENJAMIN CLARK was recently reported to the Secretary as living in Texas, but his address is not yet received.

*RANDOLPH MARSHALL CLARK, after serving as First Lieutenant in the First Massachusetts Cavalry, was transferred to the Second Massachusetts Cavalry, receiving a captain's commission. His health had been so undermined by camp life that the surgeon of the regiment refused to give him a certificate, and he was thus prevented from joining the regiment. This was a bitter disappointment, as he had cherished a hope of serving in the army to the end of the war.

He visited Europe many times, travelling extensively in Norway and Sweden, and making a second extended trip through Russia, visiting the Crimea and writing letters for the press, which were widely copied. He wrote several lectures on Russia, particularly Moscow and the Crimea, which he delivered before various societies. He had the financial charge of a large mill, of which his father was chief owner, and also the exclusive charge of his father's affairs during a protracted absence in Europe. He was devotedly attached to the church of his choice (the Protestant Episcopal), working zeal-ously in her various organizations and filling positions of responsi-bility. He died suddenly at his father's house in Dedham, Sept. 11, 1873, of heart disease, leaving a widow and two daughters, the eldest of which is Eleanor Vinton, born March 30, 1867; the younger, Ethel Randolph, born June 6, 1870.

He left an ample estate for his family. His widow is living in Pomfret, Conn., where she has a beautiful estate. She has spent some time in Europe since his death, for the better education of her children.

THOMAS WILLIAM CLARKE is in active practice at the Suffolk Bar. He has made specialties of patent and copyright law. He is, especially in the latter department, one of the authorities in this country. He has written an essay on the Steam Power of Massachusetts for the Census Bureau of this State, which is pub-lished in the Superintendent's report. This essay has been highly praised by Prof. Bowen as a politico-economical contribution to general knowledge on this subject. One newspaper called it " gorgeous in diction," and another " brilliant and complete," while it impressed a third " as a choice and novel production " This great man has found much refreshment, during his hours of ease, in teaching the boys and girls of his neighborhood to ride. He is saved from astonishing revelations solely by his prompt repentance and reformation at half past eleven, after the receipt of the Secre-tary's second circular.

GEORGE GORDON CROCKER. When last heard of, Crocker was living somewhere in the South.

JOSEPH MACKENZIE CUSHING still resides in Baltimore, and is a member of the firm of Cushings & Bailey. When last heard from, he was unmarried.

CHARLES AUGUSTUS CUTTER has made a great reputation as a bibliographer. His material children are Philip Champney, born at Cambridge, Nov. 5, 1866; Roland Norcross, born at the same place, July 28, 1868. His handwriting is of the meanest description; but, when you get at the contents, your labors are repaid. He has forgotten how to spell, however. His intellectual children consist of many notes in the *Nation;* a letter in the *Nation* of Feb. 8, 1877, in reply to Prof. Hagen, who, intending to attack the system of cataloguing used at Harvard College, had criticised the American ideas of cataloguing in general. Cutter continued this subject in the *Library Journal*, Vol. I., pages 216 to 220. Cutter has edited the department bibliographical (spelt with an " f ") in the *Library Journal*, from its foundation in 1876. He has contributed many articles, communications, and notes to the *Library Journal*. He has published a most valuable set of rules for a dictionary catalogue, which he graciously has sent to the Secretary, who now waits for his other classmates to furnish the dictionaries. He also made the catalogue for the Winchester town library, and has brought the catalogue of the Boston Athenæum down to the letter " S." He has continued to be the librarian of the Boston Athenæum ever since 1865. He attended the conference of librarians in London, Oct. 2 to 5, 1877, and made a week's visit in Paris. In his old age, he has become gay, not to say frivolous. He has taken considerable part, of late, not only in social and literary clubs, but has absolutely joined in private theatricals. He is engaged in the preparation of a general system of classification of books on the shelves, to be used primarily in the Athenæum, but also intended for use elsewhere. This he is about to publish, and will give in it his own novel plan of notation. In 1877 he removed from Cambridge to Winchester.

He is respectfully referred to old Major Pendennis (1 Pen. Thack. 75), — "What! love a woman who spells affection with only one ' f '? "

*EDWARD BARRY DALTON died in California, on May 13, 1872. With his career as Medical Director of the Army of the Potomac we are all familiar. He tendered his resignation to the adjutant general on April 24, 1865, for the reason "that, as the necessity for volunteer medical officers in the army was no longer pressing, he wished to turn his attention to private business." His resignation was accepted, with the recommendation that he receive the thanks of the War Department for meritorious services. On Aug. 15, 1865, he received, for "faithful and meritorious services," brevets of Lieutenant-Colonel and Colonel.

He spent the summer in rest, and returned to his profession in New York City, where, in September, 1865, he formed a medical copartnership with Dr. George A. Peters, which continued for several years with entire pleasure to both parties.

In March, 1866, Dalton's genius for executive work was again called into exercise by his being chosen the chief executive officer of the Metropolitan Board of Health for New York, Brooklyn, and the adjacent country. His title was "Sanitary Superintendent," and he organized a corps of twenty-four inspectors and thirty-seven assistants for this work. The complete result of his efficient services is found in the account of the work accomplished by the Board, which is given in an article written by Dalton in the *North American Review* for April, 1868. Gradually, however, the control of the Board became an instrument for party management, and Dalton retired from his office in January, 1869, because he would not lend himself to such arts.

He had been during this period clinical assistant to the Professor of Medicine in the New York College of Physicians and Surgeons, and lecturer on nervous diseases in the summer session, and visiting physician to several private charities and hospitals.

In 1868, he lost his only child, an infant daughter of less than a year in age.

In 1869, his wife died in confinement, and shortly afterwards his own health gave way, and he was entirely disabled by an attack of latent pleurisy. He was long an invalid, and obliged to withdraw from active business. He travelled in Europe during this period; and in October, 1869, he returned to Boston, and became visiting physician to the Massachusetts General Hospital, and instructor in the theory and practice of medicine in the Medical College. But not for long. In October, 1871, he was forced again to travel for his health, and visited California in hope that the milder climate of the Pacific coast might still prolong his usefulness. He established himself in the neighborhood of Santa Barbara, where he had nearly completed his arrangements for purchasing a farm; but in the following spring he again failed and never rallied. Members of his family were with him when he died, on May 13, 1873.

A friend who knew him well says:—

" I never shall forget the tender grace of his home in the midst of that great hospital near City Point. Living in the midst of thousands of wounded and the sick, his wife was with him, and they both seemed like angels of mercy to soothe the pains of war."

As blow after blow came upon him and shattered his earthly hopes, he exhibited the spirit which he had taught us to expect of him. Patient, cheerful, brave, he died, as he had lived, a noblehearted gentleman.


GEORGE DEXTER, from 1866 to 1871, spent the greater part of each year in New Orleans. In 1872 he married Miss S. R. Endicott, of Salem, and was in Europe during 1872–3. He returned to this country in the autumn of 1873, and has since resided in Longwood. He was for many years engaged in buying cotton; but in 1877 he accepted the treasurership of the Pepperell and Laconia Cotton Mills. He has one son, born in October, 1874, at Longwood. He gives the Secretary good advice not to wait for residuary bequests, but to get what money he can out of the class now for class-scholarship funds. The Secretary proposes to follow that advice.

JOHN W. EDGERLY still lives at Ottumwa, Iowa. His children are as follows: Edward Tyler, born Jan. 15, 1864; Adeline Chambers, born Dec. 6, 1866; John Woods, Jr., born Aug. 20, 1868; Alice Louise, born October 15, 1870; Ellen Maria, born Nov. 21, 1872; George E., born July 23, 1877. His eldest son is now attending Phillips Academy, at Exeter, and proposes to enter Freshman at Harvard in 1881. Edgerly continued in the hardware business in Ottumwa until 1873. He then purchased stock in the Iowa National Bank of that place; was elected Vice-President at that time, and, shortly afterwards, on the resignation of the former cashier, became cashier, which office he still holds. He has been a member of the Board of Education in Ottumwa for about twelve years, and for most of that time has been President of the Board.

* PAYSON PERRIN ELLIS died at Shanghae, China, Sept. 26, 1863.

JAMES A. EMMERTON was marked out for a distinguished career in charge of the insane. He has consequently stuck very closely to Salem, and the neighborhood of his old chum. He is thought to have preserved him from delirium of many kinds; but all his efforts have been insufficient to prevent Waters and Ropes from sinking into lethargy when the writing of a letter is suggested.

* LANGDON ERVING died in Baltimore on May 20, 1862.

ALFRED DOUGLAS EVANS, early in the war of the Rebellion, was paymaster on a United States vessel. After the capture of New Orleans, he was employed in government service in the custom-house or revenue office at that port till about 1869, when he went to Austin, Texas, and there became connected with the land office till about 1872. In that year he returned to Boston, and, with the exception of one year spent in Europe, was there occupied as a conveyancer till 1877. In that year he removed to Corpus Christi, Texas, where he now resides. He has never been married.

WILLIAM HENRY EVANS was for some years settled in Holyoke, Mass., but resigned about a year ago, and is at present in Cambridgeport. He has been a diligent student in his profession, and is said to have displayed unusual vigor as a theological writer and speaker.

HENRY SIDNEY EVERETT has been for some years in the diplomatic employment of the United States, and is residing abroad.

FRANK WILLIAM FISKE is a prosperous merchant in Buffalo. Being detained by a railroad breakdown for a few hours in that city last winter, the Secretary called at his house, and finding Fiske absent, spent the evening in narrating to his children the pranks of their father in college. He took the precaution to leave just before that father returned, and has not again ventured to stop in Buffalo.

EDWIN AUGUSTUS GIBBENS has for many years conducted a successful school for boys in the city of New York. His present location is opposite the Windsor Hotel, on Fifth Avenue. Before going to New York, he resided in Waltham for several years, in charge of the New Church School in that place. He has several children.

JOHN GREEN, in July, 1865, was living in Boston, practising medicine when people would let him, and supposing himself fixed there for life. In November of that year he "pulled up stakes in Boston to drive them anew in St. Louis, where they still stick fast." He spent the winter of 1865 and 1866 in Europe, and in the summer of 1866 began making diseases of the eye his specialty. He married, Oct. 22, 1868, Harriet Louisa Jones, of Templeton, Mass., cousin of Jones on Mortgages. His children are: John, born in Templeton, Aug. 2, 1873; Elizabeth, born in St. Louis, Dec. 3, 1878.

On his regular tour the Secretary examined Green's quarters in St. Louis, which were found surrounded with a crowd of sore eyes. His own sight was so far affected that he was unable to see Green in his own home. It is unnecessary to say to any one who is familiar with the West that Green stands in the front rank of Western oculists, and is a great authority in that branch of medical practice. He informs me that he has no grandchildren as yet, but is not without hope.

CHARLES AUGUSTUS GREGORY has lived in Chicago for the last fifteen years. He had accumulated a large property before the fire. Subsequently, he was president of the Cook County Land Company. Within the last two years, he has returned to the active practice of the law in Chicago. His office is at No. 184 Dearborn Street. He has one son, Harold, who is about eleven years old.

JOSEPH GUTMAN has been for many years in New York City, one of the leading United States Commissioners. He has sat as magistrate in several of the most important extradition cases, and is said to have exported more rascals than any other man in the country. He is the proper person to take your depositions, *de bene*, in New York.

GEORGE HENRY HAMPSON. Nothing has been heard from Hampson since the last report.

JOSEPH HAYES is still engaged in business in New York City, and is president of mining companies. He has visited Colorado and South America. His present address is No. 4 Post-Office Square, Boston, Mass.

JOSEPH CONVERSE HEYWOOD has published several poems, which, for want of presentation copies, the Secretary can-not properly criticise. He is said to have lately married a wealthy widow lady in Philadelphia, and to be at present in Europe.

HENRY LEE HIGGINSON travelled in Europe during 1872. He is married to Miss Ida Agassiz, and now lives in Boston. He has been for several years a member of the firm of Lee, Higginson & Co. He has been associated with Alexander Agassiz in his copper mines, and like everybody else connected with those enterprises, has reaped a golden harvest from them, as well as from many other independent ventures of his own and of his firm.

CHARLES CUSHING HOBBS is supposed to be still residing in South Berwick practising law, and, as he last reported himself in 1865, absorbed in " maiden meditation," though " fancy free."

*GEORGE FOSTER HODGES died at Hall's Hill, near Alexandria, on Jan. 31, 1862, in the military service of the United States.

JAMES K. HOSMER. His children are: Edward Stebbins, born at Deerfield, Mass., June 1, 1876; Eliot Norton, born at Yellow Springs, Ohio, Dec. 28, 1868 (died June, 1879); Ernest Cutter, born at Yellow Springs, Ohio, July 2, 1870; Josephine, born at Columbia, Mo., March 31, 1874; Ruth, born at St. Louis, Mo., Oct. 20, 1879. He was married, for the second time, Nov. 27, 1878, to Miss Jenny P. Garland, of St. Louis.

His writings are as follows: In 1870, for the *Atlantic Monthly,* "Father Mèriel's Bell"; in 1871, "The Giant in the Spiked Helmet" (an account of Prussia); in 1872, "The New Wrinkle at Sweetbrier"; in 1876, "At Lützen." He has written for the New York *Nation,* "Our Town Nomenclature," "The Talk of the Unlettered Folk," "The Drama in Colleges" "A Famous Field" (an account of a visit to the battle-field of Hastings). He has written for the *Western* (St. Louis), "Let us be Intelligible"; "Heinrich Heine"; "A Ghost's Adventure." In 1874, he read before the National Education Association a paper on "Co-education," published in the Transactions of the Association. He has also written numerous book reviews for *Old and New,* the *Christian Register,* and the *Literary World,* writing for the latter, critiques of Boyesen's "Goethe and Schiller," and Bayard Taylor's "Sketches of German Literature." In 1878, he wrote a book entitled "A Short History of German Literature," which is exceedingly interesting and has met with great favor.

He greatly regrets that he cannot attend the dinner, and sends kind words to all.

SAMUEL JOHNSTON still resides in Chicago, where he owns vast acres of his own, and runs horse-railroads over other people's acres to his own profit. As he makes no report to the contrary, he is supposed to be married and have a family of ten children, and to be the first grandparent among us.

LEONARD A. JONES was married on the fourteenth day of December, 1867, to Josephine H. Lee, of Templeton, Mass. His only child, Arthur Lee, was born March 9, 1869, and died Oct. 18 of the same year. His publications have been as follows : In 1871, two articles in *Old and New* on " The Language of Brutes"; in 1877, an article in the *Southern Law Review* on " Power of Sale, Mortgages, and Trust Deeds"; in 1878, " A Treatise on the Law of Mortgages of Real Property," in two volumes ; also two articles in the *Southern Law Review*, the first on " The Legal Nature of Rolling-Stock of Railroads," and the second on " Receivers of Railroads"; and an article in the *American Law Review* on " Claims and Equities Affecting the Priority of Railroad Mortgages"; in 1879, a second and revised edition of " Mortgages of Real Property," above named ; also, " A Treatise on the Law of Railroad and other Corporate Securities, including Municipal Aid Bonds"; also, an article in *Southern Law Review* on " Fraudulent Mortgages of Merchandise " (afterwards published as a monograph) ; in 1880, two articles in *American Law Review* on " The Law of Corporate Securities." He is also about to publish soon " A Treatise on the Law of Chattel Mortgages," and " A Treatise on the Law of Pledges and Collateral Securities."

SAMUEL CROCKER LAWRENCE has continued to reside in Medford. Lawrence was a member of the Stockholders' Committee in the Eastern Railroad at the time of the collapse in its stock some four years ago. He was a heavy stockholder, and was chosen president of the company during its reorganization period, and was largely instrumental in bringing it into its present sound condition.

Lawrence's adopted son graduated at Harvard in 1879.

WILLIAM PITT PREBLE LONGFELLOW married Miss Emily Daniell of Boston in 1870. He was, for upwards of two years, assistant supervising architect of the United States at Washington. Then he resigned that office and travelled in Europe with his wife. On his return, he bought a house in Cambridge near his uncle, Henry W. Longfellow, where he still resides. He is the editor of the *American Architect's Journal*, and is engaged in the business of his profession.

BENJAMIN SMITH LYMAN is in Japan, where he has been making geological and mining surveys since 1873. He has now closed his work for the Mikado's government, but still remains in Japan. He has surveyed, and described in printed reports, a large part of the Japanese empire, and knows more about the countries which compose it than probably any other living white man. He has lived there exclusively for seven years, and is able to speak the language perfectly, and has, besides, traversed many of its regions where foreigners seldom go. During the year previous to going to Japan, Lyman was a mining engineer employed by the government of India upon surveys in the Punjaub. Any communications sent to the care of Miss Mary Lyman, Northampton, Mass., will be forwarded to his address. He has never been married.

CHARLES FREDERICK LYMAN continues to reside in Boston, but is not engaged in active business.

THEODORE LYMAN has lived, since the Secretary's last report, in Boston and Brookline, except from October, 1871, to August, 1873, when he travelled in Europe. There, in July, 1873, he had the sorrow to lose his daughter Cora, his only child at that time. There have been since born to him two sons: Theodore, Nov. 23, 1874, and Henry, Nov. 7, 1878.

From the time of his appointment, in 1865, he has been a Commissioner of Fisheries for Massachusetts, the first State to begin an organized effort for the cultivation and preservation of food-fishes. The movement thus started has extended to thirty-one other States and to the United States government, whose commission, furnished with a large appropriation, has carried on a series of experiments and observations of a magnitude never before attempted.

He has done something in the zoölogy of radiated animals, has taken a constant interest in our Alma Mater, and has given much attention to public charities. He is, as we all know, a bountiful and judicious giver, and never forgets old friends.

He is an Overseer of Harvard College; member of the faculty of the Museum of Comparative Zoölogy; trustee of the Peabody Museum of Archæology and of the national Peabody Education Fund; member of the Boston Society of Natural History, the American Academy of Arts and Sciences, the National Academy of Sciences, and of the Société Linnéenne de Bordeaux; and president of the Boston Farm School. His principal publications have been : —

Illustrated Catalogue of the Ophiuridæ and Astrophytidæ in the Museum of Comparative Zoölogy, 1865, with a Supplement, 1871.

Report on Ophiuridæ and Astrophytidæ dredged by L. F. de Pourtalès, 1869.

Papers relating to the Garrison Mob, 1870.

Note sur les Ophiurides et Euryales du Musée d'Histoire Naturelle de Paris, 1872.

Ophiuridæ and Astrophytidæ, old and new, 1874.

Ophiuridæ and Astrophytidæ of the "Hassler" Expedition, 1875.

Dredging Operations of the U. S. Steamer "Blake": Ophiurans, 1875.

Prodrome of the Ophiuridæ and Astrophytidæ of the "Challenger" Expedition. Part I., 1878; Part II., 1879.

All the Annual Fishery Reports of Massachusetts, from 1865 to the present year, have been wholly or in part written by him.

The class owes him much for his unflagging and generous interest in our reunions and all class affairs. Like Hodges, he never fails to remember his classmates and do his best for them.


* MALCOLM MACEUEN died several years ago in Pennsylvania.


WILLIAM MACKAY, shortly after the last report, removed to

New York, and engaged in business there. He afterwards retired from business, and lived a considerable time abroad. Returning with his family to this country, he resided for a year in Cambridge, and now lives in Southboro', Mass.

WILLIAM SLIDELL McKENZIE, although one would not have thought it of him, repented and reformed at the eleventh hour, and then endeavored to soothe the Secretary's feelings by addressing him as "that once mild youth." In 1865, McKenzie was the pastor of a church in Providence, R. I., where he had been settled since the opening of the year 1860. His health, however, broke down under the severe pressure of work. He was obliged to resign his pastorate and seek rest. Under medical advice, he took his family, then consisting of his wife and two children, and went to New Brunswick, where he bought a horse, and pitched his tent on the banks of the Mirimachi River. At the end of a year his health was completely restored. Although he does not confess it, this result was undoubtedly attained by a sort of Friar-Tuck life, profuse indulgence in salmon-fishing and venison in that delightful region. He is reported to have strolled through the forests with a breech-loader, and, in the intervals of theological reflection, to have brought down many a fine buck. The natives preserve traditions that he dropped his meditations and the buck every time that animal appeared. But McKenzie struggled with his natural man, overcame his unhallowed love of field sports, and, returning to civilization, was again settled as a pastor in the city of St. John, N. B., where he preached until the summer of 1872, and also assisted in the publication of a weekly religious journal. During this period, however, the original Adam was strong within him. He actually, even now in his subdued state, takes pride in the remembrance that he plunged his paper into several long and heated controversies on various topics. He got people generally together by and on their ears, and received his full share of hard names and abuse, as he says; but probably did not get his full deserts. Several sheets took up cudgels against him; and, although he cheerfully says that this was fun to him, it is understood that its results were deadly to his adversaries. He left St. John, and, doubtless on account of his fighting qualities, was made the secretary for the District of

New England in connection with the Baptist Missionary Union, which has general charge of the Baptist missions over the world. McKenzie is thought to have tackled the great Adversary very successfully *in partibus infidelium.* In addition to his duties as secretary, he has conducted the editorial work of the society's missionary periodical. His office is in the Tremont Temple, in Boston. His home is in the town of Winchester, about eight miles from Boston. He frequently travels through New England, and disburses each year about $300,000 in the work of his society. McKenzie has six children, to wit: J. W. Merrill, THE CLASS BABY, Lizzie Stanwood, Charles Fisk, Maud Cranston, Andrew Comstock, and Anna Knight. The class did well in giving McKenzie a substantial class cradle; and he has done well in filling it. Although, it is true, the Secretary, being then unmarried and without experience, delivered the cradle without any mattress or bedding, and left the first-born progeny of the class to sleep on the slats, this arrangement seems to have proved salutary. The class baby was born in Andover, July 11, 1858; but as McKenzie confesses that his family Bible is not at hand, he does not know when the rest were born, but is sure of the great fact. The class baby, when about ready to enter college, was seized with a mania for going to sea. He doubled Cape Horn, but was satisfied with one voyage. He is now employed in a manufacturing establishment in Boston, AND IS MARRIED. He keeps house in Chelsea, and, his father says, is raising a family, and regretting every day that he did not go to college. His father expects him to chew the cud of repentance all his days. The information of the Secretary is not definite on the point, but, according to the best of his knowledge, information, and belief, it is a fairly open question whether McKenzie has not had the GRAND CLASS BABY also. *If this is so*, the class ought to make a special appropriation to get bedding to cover the slats of the class cradle.

In 1873, Lagrange College, in Missouri, added a D. D. to McKenzie's name. He says he does not know why the title was given him, and is equally ignorant how to shake it off. The great success upon which he prides himself in life is in keeping all his bills paid; and truly, in so doing, he excites the envy of some of his classmates who have not done so much. He says that his interest in the class grows stronger every year.

GEORGE FREDERICK McLELLAN was busy, from 1861 to 1868, practising law in Washington, D. C., with good success, until his health became impaired by overwork. From 1868 to 1874 he was president of the Board of Education of the district, and labored energetically in improving the public schools. By direction of his physician, he then removed to Los Angeles, Cal., where he is now engaged in the insurance business, and finds his health thoroughly restored He writes that his children are all unborn, and likely to remain in that blest condition of innocence ; and that he would be " glad to have his hair stand on end if it would only come back." He sends cordial remembrances to the class.

CHRISTOPHER BRIDGE MARSH has remained in the employment of the Cincinnati, Hamilton and Dayton Railway Company, the office of which is in Cincinnati, O. On Nov. 3, 1869, he was married to Carolynne Denison Disney. His children are: Richard Disney, born March 25, 1873, at Connorsville, Ind. ; Pearson Fessendon, born June 25, 1875, at Glendale, O. ; William Hunt, born April 14, 1877, at Glendale, O. For the last five years he has been living in Glendale, about fifteen miles from Cincinnati. Marsh is cashier of the company, and means to come to the dinner. He says he is the only member of the class in Ohio.

* WILLIAM WARD MERIAM was murdered by Turkish robbers on July 3, 1862, while residing as missionary at Philippopolis.

JAMES TYNDALE MITCHELL has been hard at work in the law, since 1865, in Philadelphia. In 1871 he was elected to the bench of the District Court of Philadelphia, a court of general original jurisdiction, both at law and in equity, in all cases involving more than five hundred dollars. This position he still holds, except that, in 1875, the name of the court was changed to the Court of Common Pleas. Since 1862 he has been the chief and responsible editor of the *American Law Register*, which is well known in the profession as second in importance and influence to no other law journal in the country. It is said to have the largest 'ation and the widest' distribution of all the law periodicals.

Its success is largely due to the learning and skill which Mitchell has displayed in its conduct. Besides his editorial work, he has published an edition of " Williams on Real Property," with American notes, several pamphlets on legal subjects, and performed a good deal of miscellaneous legal work. He is still unmarried. His office is No. 229 South Sixth Street, Philadelphia. He is our only judge, the *rara avis* referred to in the Secretary's first circular.

EDWIN MORTON was residing in Plymouth in 1865, and practising as a lawyer in that vicinity. In 1868 he came to Boston, where he maintained an office until 1874, when he left for a voyage around the world. He was in California in 1875 ; in India, Egypt, and Greece in 1876 ; and has since that time resided, for the benefit of his health, at Baden, in Switzerland, at a water-cure hotel. His health, as the Secretary is informed, is not greatly improved, nor does it seem likely to be much worse. He is not married, and is not known to have written any books or magazine articles since he left Boston.

ROBERT TREAT PAINE followed the law, with good pecuniary reward, until May, 1870. He then revisited Europe for four months, and decided to retire from active practice and seek the future occupation of his life in things relating to the welfare of the laboring and poorer classes. Since then he has been engaged in making experiments and efforts to that end. He has built numerous small tenement houses for mechanics, and taken an active part in the management of the Co-operative Building Company, which has erected, renovated, and purified a great many homes for the laboring men in the vicinity of Boston. He has actively worked in the Episcopal City Mission among the Boston poor. He is the president of the recently established society, entitled " The Associated Charities of Boston." Any one who wishes to understand this most judicious and effective form of charity organization, admirably planned and as admirably administered, should apply to Paine for a copy of his address, delivered at the Charity Building, Chardon Street, Boston, March 12, 1879. In this pamphlet, Paine has explained and discussed its principles and object, which is to raise

6

the needy above the need of relief, rather than to give alms. His treatment of the subject shows all that ability which we have a right to expect from our associate first-scholar.

Paine is also president of the Wells Memorial Workingmen's Club and Institute for the workingmen of Boston.

Paine was a member of the Building Committee of Trinity Church, over which Phillips Brooks is the rector. For nearly three years much of his time and thought was absorbed in his duties upon the committee, which reared this magnificent structure. Fine as it is, however, it is no more than a fitting place for the religious services which are held in it, and it is become the spiritual home of multitudes of the poor, as well as of the rich.

Paine has had seven children, six of whom are still living : namely, Edith, born April 6, 1863, in Boston ; Fanny, born Jan. 13, 1865, in Boston ; Robert Treat, born April 9, 1866, in Waltham ; Florence, born Sept. 30, 1868, in Waltham, and died July 17, 1872 ; Ethel, born March 24, 1872, in Boston ; George Lyman, born April 29, 1874, in Waltham ; Lydia Lyman, born Sept. 6, 1876.

* STEPHEN GEORGE PERKINS was killed in the battle of Cedar Mountain, Virginia, Aug. 9, 1862.

WILLIAM DEAN PHILBRICK resides at Newton Centre, Mass. He is father of nine children. They are : Arthur, born Nov. 26, 1864 ; John Dean, born Oct. 13, 1866 ; Eliza, born May 9, 1868 ; Anna Decatur, born Sept. 11, 1869 ; James Staigg, born Nov. 14, 1870 ; Helen, born March 5, 1871 ; Mary, born Aug. 3, 1872 ; Margaret, born Dec. 24, 1874 ; Miriam, born July 18, 1876. His occupation is gardening. He has written several prize essays on gardening for the Massachusetts Board of Agriculture and the Massachusetts Horticultural Society, and has made numerous contributions to the agricultural press.

WILLIAM QUINCY PHILLIPS has, since 1865, resided most of the time abroad. When in this country, his home is still in Cambridge, in the hospitable mansion of his late father, Judge Willard Phillips, as many of his classmates well know.

EDWARD S. RAND, Jr., practised law, especially convey-ancing, in Boston, for some years. He also gave great attention to botany, and published several books, particularly in reference to the cultivation of flowers and horticulture. He was married on Nov. 23, 1858, to Miss Jennie Augusta Lathrop, of Dedham. His children are: Edward L., born Aug. 22, 1859; Henry L., born Jan. 1, 1862; Jennie A., born Oct. 21. 1868; and Percy A., born Aug. 20, 1872. For the last few years he has been in Brazil.

JAMES REED. James Reed is still pastor of the Church of the New Jerusalem in Boston, the largest Swedenborgian society in the world. In addition to the four children named in my last report, he has the following: Joseph S., born Oct 25, 1868; and Emily E., born Feb. 21, 1876. His daughter Miriam died March 17, 1876, at the age of eleven years. He has published three books: namely, " Religion and Life," in 1868; " Man and Woman, Equal but Unlike," in 1870; and " Swedenborg and the New Church," in 1880. His eldest son, John, is on a voyage to Eastern Africa.

The hearts of his people turn to him with constant affection; and his peaceful life is the natural fruit of his boyhood as we all knew it.

WILLIAM WHITING RICHARDS is said to have a school in New York, and to reside in Hackensack, New Jersey. He is a criminally bad correspondent, and evidently unable to teach boys to write even English. Riddle says his address is No. 723 Sixth Avenue, New York; but it is of no use to write to it. He has five children, William Milliken, Lowell Lincoln, Bessie, Gertie, and Frank.

WILLIAM QUINCY RIDDLE has continued in the practice of law in New York. He will be with us at the dinner. He wrote to the Secretary a long letter, full of good-will, but without a particle of information in it, and not even mentioning his address.

NATHANIEL ROPES lives in Salem, where he has resided for many years. He is supposed to be unmarried, and engaged in tak-ing care of his property and Waters and Emmerton.

ANTOINE RUPPANNER has practised medicine with success in the city of New York for many years. He lived for a long time at the Fifth Avenue Hotel, and now makes his home at the Windsor. He has also become a capitalist, and his name is mighty on Wall Street. He knows that Burgundy ought to lie down in a basket, and not be shaken up for human imbibition. He makes railroad tours over the country, in order to pick up profitable investments. He was, when last heard of, travelling in style to San Francisco in a private car. The impecunious members will do well to put him through a financial cross-examination as to his private fancies in bonds, when he appears at the dinner-table.

He is also president of the Goethe Club; and it was the Secretary's fortune to hear him last winter advise a patient that to consult one physician was dangerous, that to employ two was almost certainly fatal, while three in consultation invariably produced sudden death. His criticism filled the hearers with profound respect for his pocket, and strengthened their faith in homœopathic pills.

* EDWARD GRENVILLE RUSSELL was, shortly before the issuance of our first circular last March, thrown down by a runaway horse, and his brain so injured that he did not recover consciousness while he lived. He died on Feb. 24, 1880. His funeral took place from the First Parish Church in Cambridge. Dr. Peabody officiated at the church. The services at the house were conducted by the Rev. J. P. Bland, who also assisted at the church. Various societies, of which Russell was a member, were in attendance to pay the last tribute of respect to his memory. His grave is on Fountain Avenue, No. 4001, Mt. Auburn Cemetery. Russell was always regular in attendance at our meetings, and it is said that he looked forward with great pleasure to being present this year, and intended to have written something to be read to the class. His home was No. 343 Harvard Street, Cambridge. The following sketch is furnished by his wife for insertion here: —

" He was one of the best known citizens of Cambridge, he having resided for many years in that city. He has written several essays for the public press, and also several poems. He was born at Groton, Mass., June 2, 1834, prepared for college at Phillips

Academy, Exeter, N. H., and entered Harvard College in 1851. He graduated in 1855, with the degree of A. M., and immediately entered the Divinity School, from which he graduated in 1858. He obtained a license to preach from the Boston Association of Ministers the same year, and shortly after was ordained as an Evangelist at Groton Junction. now Ayer. He was never assigned to any regular parish, but filled many pulpits acceptably, and further performed services as minister at large.

" He was married, in Cambridge, Feb. 22, 1860, to Miss Mary A. Stewart, by the Rev. Caleb Davis Bradlee.

" He held several offices of importance and influence, the duties of which he performed to the acceptance of those whom he served. He was Justice of the Peace, Notary Public, Commissioner to Qualify Civil Officers, and Commissioner of Deeds for the States of Maine, New Hampshire, Vermont, Massachusetts, Rhode Island, and Connecticut. He was a prominent Democrat, and a candidate of the party for several prominent positions He was connected with and a prominent member of the following bodies: Mt. Olivet Lodge, F. A. M., of Cambridge; Miller Royal Arch Chapter, Franklin, Mass.; Cryptic Council, R. and S. Masters, Newtonville; Gethsemane Commandery, K. of P., Newtonville; Lafayette Lodge of Perfection, Boston; Giles Y. Yates Council of P. of S, Boston; Friendship Lodge, I. O. O. F., of Cambridgeport; Charles River Encampment, I. O. O. F.; the Grand Encampment, of Boston; Mystic Lodge, K. of P., Natick Section; and of the Grand Lodge, of Boston. He was connected with the New England Historic Genealogical Society, Boston; member of the German Rifle Club, National Lancers, and the Massachusetts Guards, of Boston He had insurance certificates, issued by six Masonic bodies, five Odd Fellows, and three Knights of Pythias Lodges. He also had a policy in the New England Life Insurance Company, of Boston. He was interested in real estate, to which he devoted much time, the balance of which was absorbed in the manifold duties connected with the bodies of which he was an active member, and in which he held positions requiring ability and skill of a high order, and for which he had special qualifications. He was at several times presented with jewels and regalias. He delivered a lecture on 'Odd

Fellowship' before Friendship Lodge, in 1874, which was considered one of the most brilliant ever presented before that justly celebrated body.

" He was a lover of the German language, and frequently contributed translations to the press. He was the compiler of a key to 'Fosse's Spanish Grammar,' indorsed by Prof. S. C. Bello, Spanish Instructor of Harvard College, and as a writer and speaker won renown. He prepared, and there will be given to the public, a volume of his writings in prose and poetry."

GEORGE PEABODY RUSSELL is one of the trustees under the will of his uncle, the late George Peabody, of London, and is supposed to give his whole time to the administration of the charities which that will created. He never suffered any permanent ill effects from being drowned while bathing in the Connecticut River during his Sophomore year at Dartmouth; while the resolutions which we sorrowfully passed in his honor at our class-meeting (prior to his arrival at it) have done him good service ever since as a permanent certificate of moral character. They are understood to have been the foundation of his late uncle's confidence in him, and to have been a chief cause of his being made a trustee of the girls' school at Bradford and his designation to his present responsible office.

FRANKLIN B. SANBORN cannot be with us at the dinner. He pledged himself to attend the Conference of Charities in Cleveland, O., on the same day, before he knew of the date of our meeting. In 1865, he was secretary of the Massachusetts Board of State Charities, by the appointment of Governor Andrew. In October of that year, at a meeting over which Governor Andrew presided, he assisted in organizing the American Social Science Association, of which he was one of the secretaries, until 1868; and has been, since 1873, the sole chief secretary. He has played an important part in the maintenance of that important organization. In 1874, he called together the first Conference of Charities, and has had much to do with establishing this institution on a sound basis. He has written several of its publications, and gives its history in two reports in the social economy department. In 1866 and 1867, Sanborn called the meeting out of which grew the Massachusetts Infant Asylum, which our classmate, Theodore Lyman, some years later, so generously endowed. This is one of the most successful institutions in existence for the preservation of infant life, where the father and mother have deserted their offspring. Sanborn was one of its first directors, and largely concerned in its active management, until he removed to Springfield in 1868. In 1866 and 1867, Sanborn helped to found the Clarke Institution for Deaf-Mutes, which first made successful the teaching of articulation to deaf children in New England. Sanborn has been for two years president of this institution, and has seen it grow from a school of ten or twelve to a school of eighty, with a national reputation. In these works, and almost all of his charitable enterprises, he labored with his old friend, Dr. Samuel G. Howe. He succeeded Dr. Howe, in 1870, as chairman of the Board of State Charities in Massachusetts; and in that position, made, in 1875, a searching investigation into the abuses of the Tewksbury Almshouse. Dr. Howe died while this investigation was pending; but after his death Sanborn succeeded in pressing through his project, and caused the establishment to be reconstructed medically and morally, to the great comfort of many hundreds of poor people. In 1877, Sanborn was engaged in the investigation then made of the Danvers Hospital and the Westboro' Reform School, and effected important reforms in them both. In 1878 and 1879, in co-operation with Gov. Talbot and others, he reorganized the whole system of Massachusetts State charities, with special reference to the care of children and insane persons; and, in July, 1879, became Inspector of Charities under the new board, then established by the State of Massachusetts. Since that time he has been devoting himself particularly to the administration of our lunacy system, which has grown into very great importance. He visits Cleveland at this time, especially with a view to present that matter to the National Conference, and to bring about the concert of national action. He has steadily endeavored to reform the discipline of our American prisons. In company with the late Dr. Wines, he wrote a general report on that subject for the International Congress held at London in 1872, and in Stockholm in 1878, though he was unable personally to attend at either place. His essays on the prison question would make a volume of considerable size, while his other writings — literary, philanthropic, and statistical — would, if brought together, make over half a dozen volumes. In 1868, he was one of the editors of the Springfield *Republican*, and as a journalist, has written on almost every considerable literary, historical, philosophical, and political topic. He has been a frequent contributor to the *Atlantic* and *Scribner's* monthlies, the *Nation*, the *Commonwealth*, the *Independent*, the Boston *Herald*, and other newspapers. For five or six years past, he has been occupied in writing the life, and compiling letters of John Brown, of Kansas and Harper's Ferry, and expects to publish the book in 1881. In concert with Mr. Alcott, Prof. Harris, and others, he has helped to establish the Concord Sumner School of Philosophy, which is now in its second year. Sanborn is the secretary, and one of the lecturers. This undertaking promises to become a permanent institution. In February, 1865, Sanborn's first son was born. He is now a student at Phillips', Exeter, Academy, where his father was fitted for college. His second son, Victor Channing, was born April 24, 1867, and is now in the Concord High School. His third and youngest son, F. B. Sanborn, Jr., was born Feb. 5, 1871.

Sanborn lived in Springfield for four years, from 1868 to 1872. Since leaving Springfield he has resided at Concord, where he has built a charming house on Concord River, and named it "Ariana." He takes possession of it on his return from Cleveland. His office in Boston is at the State House.

* CHARLES FREDERICK SANGER died in Brooklyn not long after the last report was published.

GEORGE CARLETON SAWYER is still in charge of the Utica Academy, at Utica, N. Y. His professional engagements prevent his attending the dinner. His only son died some time ago, and the grief for his loss is ever fresh. Sawyer writes, very feelingly, his remembrances to his classmates, and desires " his cheerful greeting and liveliest remembrances to be presented to the class of 1855 from one who cherishes its dear associations."

* SAMUEL RINGGOLD SCHLEY became a member of the Roman Catholic Church, and died near Baltimore many years ago.

GEORGE MANY SEAWELL was, when last heard of, still practising law in the city of San Francisco.

CHARLES FRANCIS STONE is engaged in the practice of law in New York City, in the firm of Porter, Lowrey, Soren, and Stone, No. 2 Broad Street.

EDWARD PAYSON THWING has lived in Brooklyn since 1874, and has published a number of sermons and tracts; was recently minister of the Church of the Covenant in that city; was formerly of the Tabernacle Lay College, in Brooklyn; published a lecture, entitled "Walks About Paris"; a duodecimo volume, entitled "Preacher's Cabinet," or, "Thwing's Handbook of Illustrations." He has given considerable attention to elocution, and published "Thwing's Drill-Book in Vocal Culture and Gesture." He sends me his "Golden Wedding Ode." He married Miss Susan M. Waite, of Portland, Maine. His children are, Grace, Clarence, Eugene, Edward Waite, and Gertrude. He has lost five children by death. He is associate editor of the *Homiletic Monthly*. He does not furnish the dates of his children's birth, but is known to have had triplets, at least once.

JOHN B. TILESTON was married to Miss Mary W. Foote, of Salem, Mass., Sept. 25, 1865. His children are: Mary W., born at Salem, July 7, 1866; Margaret H., born at Salem, Nov. 1, 1867; Roger E., born at Winchester, Aug. 7, 1869; Amelia P., born at Dorchester, Oct. 30, 1872; and Wilder, born at Concord, Jan. 22, 1875. He was engaged in bookselling and publishing in the firm of Brewer & Tileston until 1870. Being then out of health, he withdrew from business and travelled for two years in Sandwich Islands and California. He then became treasurer of the savings bank in Dorchester, and held that office from 1872 to 1874. Since 1874, he has lived upon his farm near Concord, Mass.

WILLIAM HOSMER SHAILER VENTRES has lived at Peterboro', N. H., where he is said to be engaged in farming. He is reported to have seven children.

* ISAAC PARKER WAINWRIGHT lived in Boston, in feeble health and out of active employment, for some time after the issue of the last report. He died in that city several years ago, suddenly.

HENRY WALKER has remained in Boston in the practice of law. He was License Commissioner for the city of Boston during the years 1877 and 1878, and is now chairman of the Board of Police Commissioners of that city, having been appointed to hold office for three years, from May 1, 1879. He is still unmarried.

The Secretary's autobiographical information from this gentleman is limited, as he writes that he is in fear of the author officially. "Once before you invited this fly into your parlor. I gave you what you asked for, and was in truth shocked at the result." The Secretary forbears, out of mercy to the writer, to quote the remainder of the sentence from Walker's letter.

He thinks he has had no very remarkable experience since our last report. Has travelled all over the continent, from Berkshire to the Rocky Mountains, and from the Gulf to the St. Lawrence. He has been the treasurer of a church for ten years, the funds of which he still holds. He has also been an official in two or three charitable and ornamental associations.

HENRY FITZ GILBERT WATERS is said to be much devoted to antiquarian pursuits, and resides in Salem. The air of that town seems to be unfavorable to intellectual activity. Ropes, Emmerton, and Waters have forgotten their learning, and presumedly do not understand the optative mood any longer. The Secretary has no evidence that Waters and Ropes have not lost the ability to write; and he fears they could not even read his late courteous favors.

WALTER HENRY WILD. Nothing has been heard about Wild since 1865.

JOSEPH WILLARD has been engaged in the practice of law in Boston for the last fifteen years, and in writing on topics in real-estate law. His office is at Room 8, No. 33 School Street, Boston; and his house, No. 30 Staniford Street.

SMITH WRIGHT has continued in the firm of J. B. Clapp & Son, real-estate brokers, whose office now is at 198 Washington Street, Boston. Wright has three children living: Francis Newton, born before 1865 ; Arthur Sidney, born Aug. 12, 1866 ; Charles Conrad, born Nov. 27, 1871. On the 10th of May, 1872, he established himself and family at 13 Berwick Park, where he still resides. The Secretary's first circular created in his mind a wholesome dread, and produced a prompt reply. He has the ideas of an intelligent layman in dreading the effect which twenty years' legal experience might produce, if exerted upon him.

* ANDREW LAMMEY YONGUE was killed by an accident on the Charlotte and South Carolina Railroad, at Columbia, S. C., on Nov. 17, 1859.